MAMA'S HOME

written by
Shay Youngblood

illustrated by
Lo Harris

MAKE ME A WORLD
New York

Gratitude

To Christopher Myers and his vision for Make Me a World, and my editor, Michelle Frey, for great conversations about this book and her childhood favorites. Thanks to so many among my tribe who comforted me with food, sanctuary, unexpected mail, laughter, and gentle nudges in the right direction. Thank you, friends, for sharing your mothers with me when my original Big Mamas were no longer around. Grateful to the many places that have supported me and my work, including the Yaddo artist community and the cities of Atlanta, New York, and D.C. Special thanks to the librarians at the Woodridge Neighborhood Library in Northeast D.C., the Brooklyn Public Library, and the Mildred L. Terry Public Library in my hometown of Columbus, Georgia, where I developed a lifelong love of books and librarians. —S.Y.

MAKE ME A WORLD is an imprint dedicated to exploring the vast possibilities of contemporary childhood. We strive to imagine a universe in which no young person is invisible, in which no kid's story is erased, in which no glass ceiling presses down on the dreams of a child. Then we publish books for that world, where kids ask hard questions and we struggle with them together, where dreams stretch from eons ago into the future and we do our best to provide road maps to where these young folks want to be. We make books where the children of today can see themselves and each other. When presented with fences, with borders, with limits, with all the kinds of chains that hobble imaginations and hearts, we proudly say—no.

Visit us on the Web! rhcbooks.com

Educators and librarians, for a variety of teaching tools, visit us at RHTeachersLibrarians.com

Library of Congress Cataloging-in-Publication Data is available upon request.
ISBN 978-0-593-18022-8 (trade) — ISBN 978-0-593-18023-5 (lib. bdg.) — ISBN 978-0-593-18024-2 (ebook)

The text of this book is set in 15-point Colby Regular.
The illustrations were created using Procreate for iPad and Adobe Creative Cloud.
Book design by Nicole de las Heras

MANUFACTURED IN CHINA
10 9 8 7 6 5 4 3 2 1
First Edition

For my families, by blood, by choice, and by good luck—
you are my greatest loves.
—S.Y.

In loving gratitude to my family, the city of Bessemer,
and every auntie and godmother (by blood or by spirit)
who has breathed color and wisdom into my life.
You are seen, you are known, and you are loved.
—L.H.

My home is in a city
in a neighborhood

AIRPORT

in a white house

a brick house

a bright yellow tent

a big house

a little house

DINER

BEAUTY SALON
NEXT EXIT

a house in the shade
of an old oak tree

a blue house
with a room of
my own.

Every day after school I open a new door.
I'm lucky.
Not lucky my mother has to work late almost every day.
Sometimes she has to go away for weeks.
I'm lucky I have seven Big Mamas and seven houses,
one for every day of the week.

On Monday, Nurse Louella picks me up in her '57 Chevy. She takes the training wheels off my bike in the airport parking lot.

I fall down a few times, but pretty soon it feels like I can fly.

We make breakfast for dinner. Pancakes are my favorite. I think I want to be a pilot.

On Tuesday, Miss Zikora sings while we hang clothes on the line to dry. She teaches me songs in Spanish, French, and Igbo. "You're no songbird," she says, "but you'll get better." We laugh.

After choir practice, we eat delicious
fufu and pumpkin stew with our fingers.
I think I want to sing in my own band.

On Wednesday, Aunt Lily plays the blues on the radio and lets me beat out my math answers on pots and pans with a wooden spoon. Big Papa says it's pretty loud, so we play louder.

Aunt Lily lets me measure the ingredients for the cornbread to go with the gumbo soup. I think I want to be a chef.

On Thursday, Lil Jackie lets me play with her baby girl,

count the change from her tip jar,

and check out as many books from the library as I can carry.

We take turns reading stories of Black kings and queens to Baby Girl until she falls asleep.

Lil Jackie and me stay up until after midnight, eating chocolate bars and sipping red cherry sodas on the back porch. I think I want to write my own adventure stories.

On Friday afternoon, Miss Henry, and her lady friend, Miss Bunny,
teach me how to catch fish and grow a garden.

Fresh-caught fish and sweet tomatoes on the vine will never taste better. They say I can be in love with whoever my heart reaches out to. I think I want my heart to be big enough to love everybody who needs love.

On Saturday, I go to see Miss Pearl. I sit in a high chair in the beauty shop she owns while she braids my hair into a crown. I listen to the women tell stories about the old days.

They send me over to the café next door to pick up their orders of barbeque rib plates whenever the talk gets salty and turns to grown folks' business.

I think I want to be an entrepreneur, a fancy word for owning my own bicycle shop, restaurant, bookstore, *and* babysitting service.

On Sunday, everyone comes to the blue house with white trim, even my teacher and Miss Shirley, who delivers the mail.

STOP

BUS STOP

CITY BUS

TAXI

Lil Mama, Big Papa, Aunties, Uncles, and all the Big Mamas arrive by taxi, city bus, '57 Chevy, and tippy-toeing along in high-heel shoes, Stacy Adams, and mile-high hats.

I set the table with help from Baby Girl.

Miss Louella brought a silver tray of thin, lacy crepes, which are fancy French pancakes.

Miss Zikora brought a covered dish of groundnut stew she made with peanut butter and okra.

Miss Henry and Miss Bunny brought a bucket full of buttery trout for the grill and fresh tomatoes from their garden.

Aunt Lily brought a tower of cornbread balanced on her head.

Lil Jackie and Baby Girl brought sweet pink punch in a big fishbowl.

Miss Pearl brought platters of barbeque ribs and giant smoked turkey legs.

Big Papa showed up with desserts from the bakery: deep-dish blackberry pies, golden apple cobblers, and lemon cheesecakes.

When Mama comes home, we celebrate.

I sit in my special chair
next to Mama.

After the feast, Mama sings to me.
I lie down on soft blue sheets with tiny white stars in my little blue room in the big blue house and dream of all the places I'll go, the things I'll do, and the people I'll meet, just like Mama.

I love all my mamas and all our houses, and we all agree, there is no better feeling than when Mama's home.

Author's Note

My worldview was shaped as an only child, in a community where I felt like I was everyone's child. My birth mother died when I was very young. I was fortunate to grow up in a house with my great-grandmother, great-aunt, and grandfather during the week, had overnights with a teenager and her mother who lived two doors down, spent weekends with my great-aunt and great-uncle who lived across the street, and spent summers in Opelika, Alabama, with a maternal great-grandmother and a great-aunt.

Two of my maternal great-aunts grew up in north Georgia on a farm. When they moved to the city, Aunt Mae worked a small garden plot by the back door of the housing projects where she lived. She grew collard greens, tomatoes, and okra; on weekends she sold plates of smoky barbeque and boiled chitterlings, with sides of potato salad, candied yams, and collards out of her kitchen. Her sister, Aunt Luellen (I called her Mama), grew brightly colored gladiola, begonias, day lilies, and tea roses in a narrow strip of earth along the side of her small brick house.

The women who mothered me each gave a different perspective on how to be a Black woman. They encouraged me to explore all kinds of possibilities for spirituality, how to be resourceful, how to be generous and respectful of my elders and to respect myself. They taught me resilience, ways of loving and making a living. By the time they all became ancestors, I had begun to redefine what made a family. In what has become a family tradition, my younger cousins and their children all call me Auntie. I was inspired to write this book by the women who raised me; by my cousin Jada, who joined the Air Force and often left her daughter in the care of her mother; by my cousin Stephanie; and by my cousin Ursula, who takes care of three grandchildren after the loss of her beloved daughter.

I hope readers will make memory maps of their own communities and illustrate all the unique ways a family can take shape.

Sweet Pink Punch (also known as pink lemonade)

1 to 2 pints of strawberries or raspberries
6 large lemons
1 to 2 cups of sugar (or more, if you like)
1 big fishbowl or pitcher
6 to 8 cups of water (or club soda, if you want to get fancy)

Freeze half of the berries.
Juice 5 of the lemons. Thinly slice the smallest lemon into circles.
Add the other half of the berries and the sugar to the big fishbowl.
Smush the berries and sugar together with a large wooden spoon.
Add the lemon juice and the water. Stir until the sugar is dissolved.
Add the frozen berries.
Float the thin slices of lemons on top.